Rush

Of

Many

Waters

Also by Pauly Hart

Rush of Many Waters:

Volume Nineteen

By Pauly Hart

Contents

Saph and the Kitten

Long ago, Saph had become known as "The Emperor Without Words", and that was just how his subjects treated him. The subjects would come, one by one. It was always the mice first, due to their impertinence, and bow and grovel at his feet presenting their gifts one by one - in tears of sorrow. It was then that Saph would wake up screaming, as he always did. It was a farce, for his only reality was the Jade Dungeon and the Minotaur who kept him there.

The Minotaur's name was Jake, and it was funny that he lived in the Jade Dungeon. He had always wanted to go out and see the mountains, but no one had ever given him any heed, as he only spoke Kraken, and he never saw the Kraken anymore.

Saph had the same dream about the kitten every night. He was quite convinced that it really was a dream about kittens, but the mice were always there, ruining everything with their terrific demands. More piers into the sea, more bridges over the ant swamps, more this and more that. And they always left their disgusting gift in tiny pink vials. It was the tears of the ever-queen, long dead and forgotten.

How they had gotten those tears was beyond him and he probably shouldn't have asked, but in a dream, you never know how things will turn out. Invariably he would ask and they would always tell him: "She died in our loving embrace, and she let us eat her when she passed." Saph knew it was all lies, but they told him the same story over and over, and he became prone to believe it after a while.

And so, night after night, he would dream the ridiculous dream, and morning after morning the Minotaur would be there banging on his cage telling him to shut up. Breakfast would come, usually in the form of Crunchrocks, but there would never be anything to drink. Once, there was no breakfast, and once there were waffles. The waffles only happened once, and so every time he ate a crunchrock, he imagined delicious waffles with nice warm syrup. Seriously, even if the waffles they had served him had not been warm or delicious, and probably shouldn't have even been called waffles to begin with.

The Minotaur would then begin reading poetry to him. It was long and drawn out, but it pleased the Minotaur very much and since there was nothing better to do, he let the Minotaur drone away. On and on in his unique and strange language of the sea he would read poetry to Saph from his large orange book.

He had tried to teach the Minotaur to speak like him, but often, for his reward, there would only be a sharp prick with a trident. Soon Saph decided that the best thing to do was to nod and act as if the Minotaur's poetry was very important and rhymed very well.

The cage hung from a large chain high into the sky. He would have called it a ceiling, but since he couldn't see the top of it, there was no use, so he might as well call it the sky. The cage was round, and approximately one half a meter in diameter. It was very tall, however, and Saph could stand whenever he wanted, and did so often. When sitting, he would dangle his four legs out from the sides of the cage and hum quietly to himself.

One day, as he was humming along, the Minotaur came round, making his daily checks. He stopped and listened to Saph. Saph, of course, lost in song, had his eyes closed. Saph had never hummed with the Minotaur near before, for he feared that the monster would not like the tune, so he was quite stealthy about it. But this day, as I have said, his eyes were closed and there was nothing to do about it but do as you do when you don't know anyone else is watching. *Hum hum hum.*

What startled Saph more than anything was the fact that the Minotaur started humming along with him. And why not? The Minotaur was a huge fan of music. He even had an old Donna Summer record that he would play at night, up in his spire, when all the prisoners were either asleep or dead. Of course, he only had two records. The other one being a Donnie and Marie Osmond record, but he couldn't stand that one, and had since smashed it to pieces.

Saph, completely taken aback that the Minotaur had been listening, stopped. So the Minotaur poked him a little with his trident, and Saph began humming once again.

Moments turned into days, which promptly turned into weeks, and wouldn't you know it, before long, the Minotaur had learned all of the songs that Saph could teach him. This made the Minotaur angry, who had quickly decided that all he really wanted to do was to become a musician or perhaps see the mountains. This had made him feel good inside and filled him with a sense of purpose, even more than poetry ever did. "Jake" would be in lights at the theater, and everyone would come out to see him hum his famous tunes. He even stopped writing new poetry. Maybe he would write more poetry, one day... Once he had created songs from his old existing poetry from his big orange book. He had big plans.

Saph, if he had known about the Minotaur's aspirations, would have perhaps hesitantly told him that he was a terrible student of music and could not carry a tune in a bucket... But Saph did not speak Kraken, and so little was done.

That's all there is to tell. For all we know, Jake and Saph still hum away to this very day. There weren't any kittens in this story, sorry. Saph never got over the fact that the dream always happened in the same way, and Jake kept waking him up earlier and earlier just to be hummed to, so Saph never got to the part in the dream where the kittens appear. He knew that they would eventually, it just never happened.

Which makes me sad. I wanted to tell you about the kittens... And maybe I even wanted to tell how Saph taught the Minotaur lyrics and through that, taught him Grelch (which is what Saph spoke), and by that, convinced the Minotaur that he had a terrible job and should release all the prisoners at once. The Minotaur would have agreed and they all would have danced away into the sunset... But sadly, that is not at all what happened and I am incredibly sorry that there is not a better ending to this story.

Mark of the Priest

"Dang Theresa," Mark snorted, his coffee almost coming out of his nose, "Where did you get that?!"

Theresa drew up her left sleeve a little higher.

"Hold your phone up to this spot." She said, and moved his arm to right below the elbow.

Di-di-ding chimed the phone, and Theresa's face and ID marker popped up on his screen.

"Cool," he said, and looked at the screen. "Hey, you're 163 pounds?" He laughed.

"Stop it! Put it away!" she frowned, pawing at his phone.

He moved his arm out the way and stood up, still looking at the ID that was on his screen. There were icons - a hamburger menu and a gear icon. He tapped the hamburger menu. The three fat lines dropped down and displayed several grayed out functions. The only one available was "report."

"What happens if I report you?" he asked, a little seriously.

"Oh my gawd, don't you dare!" She stood up and came at him.

He held the phone out of her reach, laughing.

Dark Max

He rolled as the bullets whisked by his ear. So close. So very close this time. Ducking behind a crate, he heard them spatter the other side of the box like popcorn. *Pop! Pop! Pop!* He had only seen two bad guys, but maybe there were more. He whipped his head out and then ducked back. In less than a second, he had his bearings. *Zing!* More bullets. These guys weren't kidding. There were three of them. One on the right, one hidden behind a crate on the left, and a new guy had walked into view, between the trucks. Shotgun? *Naaaaah.* Too messy and loud. The Uzi ought to do the trick just fine.

He took a deep breath and jumped out, falling and rolling as he went. Facing them, he fired. *Brrrrrrrt!* The Uzi burped out and caught the one on the right first. He rolled again, blocking the view of the man between the trucks with the one on the left and the crate he was behind. The dude had ducked down when Max had fired and now cautiously popped his head back out. *Brrrrrrrt!* He no longer had a head.

Whezz! A bullet flew right by him. The man between the trucks had come around and stood there like an idiot. Legs spread apart, shoulders squared, one eye closed... Like a fool at the target range. Max almost felt sorry and he let another burst go from the Uzi to finish him off.

They had all three been three firing .45's and he wondered if they had any ammunition left. They usually never did, but he could still check the bodies. Never know when extra ammunition will come in handy. As he was going through pockets, he thought about yesterday. He had caught a ricochet in the leg and it had hurt like a thousand bees. It was kind of amazing how in just twelve hours the damage had already been repaired by those high-tech implants. And the medical rations he had applied didn't hurt the situation either. Heck, he wasn't even sore.

Dark Max Steele surveyed the damage on the battlefield behind him. Six snipers, a tank, a machine gunner's nest and a bunch of bozos like the three he had just taken out here. Done. Piece of cake. All he had left was that pesky robot and this area would be safe for the rest of the troops. He checked his inventory for the only way to take out the robot.

Proximity Mines: Two.

He grimaced. He had been hoping for a miracle as he always did. He had used up all his grenades on that tank, he had dropped the RPG after he had used it on the machine gunners. There was no way that his only two remaining mines were going to do the trick on that robot. "Holy Hurricanes!" he said to the air, "Now isn't that just like the Special Corps! All talk and no walk! Heck!"

Ooops.

He was talking out loud again. He hated talking out loud. He knew that he sounded like a fool, but nothing he had tried had ever worked. The old doc had told him not to worry about it, but it was embarrassing all the same. It was a good thing none of his buddies ever went with him to the battlefield, he would have died of shame. The Doom Robot lurked around the corner... any second now and he would activate his mines and run like hell...

And then it happened. The feeling came over him as suddenly as the slam of a door. Time stood still. Dark Max couldn't move. Literally, like suddenly he was encased in a frozen field. He hated this. Every now and again it would happen. In the middle of a fight, sometimes even mid conversation... Time would actually stand still and he would be suspended in this weird reality where nothing made sense. It never made any sense to him. When he was outside, you could still hear the birds. When he was in the cellars and under buildings, you could hear the dripping of water through the pipes... But these terrible moments, the ones that lasted forever, the moments that never moved?

He remembered exactly when it was and where it was when it had happened to him first. He was on his first mission in former Bophuthatswana, the blooming little country of South Africa terrorized by the tyrant Eugene Terre' Blanche and his brand of Neo Nazi hatred. He was glad that dude was gone. It had been a specifically long and bumpy mission. Bad guy after bad guy had bit the bullet. One by one, he had crept quietly along the coastal citadel and dispatched the minions of evil. At least that's how he saw all the bad guys: Minions of evil. But then, the time thing happened. He was seconds from entering the main compound and he had frozen outside of the gate. The front gate! Where anyone could have seen him! It was the worst five hours of his life. Because that's how long it had been. Five hours. I mean, the mission is almost over... And... Well, he had chocked it up to insanity. But still. He knew when it was coming up, when the mission would be over... He always knew. Sometimes you could just sense things. There were a couple of guys that were pretty tough, but he knew the real challenge lay around the corner. The Doom Robot. What the heck-fire kind of a name was that anyway? And when would he be able to move again?

Jeff put the large slice of pepperoni down next to the Mountain Dew. It was almost one in the morning but he didn't care. He didn't work tomorrow and the robot was the last boss anyway. He took a bite, a sip and pressed start.

New Armor

The Buccaneer pulled the almost frozen cartridge out of the machine. I t was roughly the size of his torso, creviced along the edges but surprisingly light. It had been so cold, because Dr. Fidleross had been keeping it in the cooler. He took it up and placed it on the table.

"How do I start the process?" he asked.

"What... for flight, use, or armor?" she looked across her shoulder as he studied it.

"Armor?" This had surprised him. He had been told of only two functions.

"Yes, we call it 'Full Form' or FF for short. It involves a technology we recently stole off... well no one you need to know about." She smiled.

He looked at her. "Yeah I'll bet you did, and I'm surprised you didn't use the word: 'Borrowed.' You could have avoided all moral issues effectively."

She turned all the way and faced him, looking up into his eyes. "Ha, ha ha Buck, very funny, but not at all deserved. Our morals here at the company are very highly respected, and you of all people should know that."

"Yeah whatever" he said. "Just show me how this gizmo works, and don't call me Buck. I hate it."

"Whatever you say, Buck." She turned to her computer.

Upon first glance the almost three foot long ten sided tube didn't look high tech at all. He studied the etches and grooves that ran the whole length. Upon finishing his inspection, he stood back and turned to her to see her sitting at her desk. She was punching up numbers on her computer. He waited for her to get done with her calculations. He couldn't figure out what she was working on, and the more he watched her, the more it didn't make any sense.

There was no rhyme or reason to what she was putting in, She wasn't looking at the screen, and upon closer inspection it appeared that her eyes weren't even open. "What are you doing?" he asked as she hammered away at the keypad. "Mmm? Oh, hold on a second." Type, type, type, and finally done. The screen went blank, and then a metallic bird of prey seemed to land on a golden planet. Three planetary rings circled the globe and read: Please... wait... processing. Cool, he thought. Very cool. He liked birds.

Poems

The Cow Path Revisited

One day through the wood, a cow walked home, as good cows often should.
He made a path, all bent askew. A crooked path as all cows do.

Since that time, four hundred years past, The cow, now dead created this path.
But still behind, he left his trail. And on that note, I'll hang my tale.

And so time fled, as time should do. They wandered the path. Those wandering few.
From dog and sheep, and travelers late, the path did grow and trail did make.

And many a man wandered out, and dodged and turned, and bent about.

They muttered dark curses full of wrath, because it was a crooked path!

The forest then, became a lane. Horse, buggy, and traveler made it plain.
The years passed on the swiftest of feet, and the lane then became a street.

A hundred thousand souls were led, by one poor cow, four centuries dead.
From path to trail to road to street, now bustling was this way with feet.

For a moral lesson does this teach, if i were ordained and called to preach.
Simple men repeat things already done. They only do what other men have done.

Taken from "The Cow Path"
Author Unknown
Copyright 2010 by pauly hart

Look dad i did it
I tied my shoes myself
Let's go find more
I can do it by myself
And i thought you would tie
All the shoes in the house

See dad, i'm winning
i'm smart and i am fast
let's play some more now
i'd like to be the best
And i thought we would play
All the whole night long

Here dad please fix it
i'ts broken and you're smart
You can fix anything
That i can tear apart
And I thought I would fail
But you kept me going strong

You're the only one for me
My first of all my three
And today was the first time
For me to believe in me

You're the bravest i can see
You helped me see in me
What only you could see

See dad, you're tired
Lay down your head and rest
I will be with you
just let me do the rest

And i thought you would fall away
But your trust helped me along

You sure mean the world to me
Thank you for all that you have done
And today was the first time
For me to believe in me

Contempt

I've traveled the world, talked to God most high
Seen what to see, enough for two lives
Don't what there was, then I did it again
Had a life full of goodness and a life life full of sin
I've had all there is, but what I couldn't find
Was someone to be there for the rest of my life

All that I needed but not what I want
I saw her pleading, her cold was now hot
She was the tool belt and I was the tool
She fucked me over and made me the fool
Needing a man for a reason or three
My love cost my life not even sex was for free

So I am here broken, pissed off and alone
You though that you owned me, set pick for the zone
But I'm not the liar, that job is all you
I still know what I want, only you are confused
You didn't want me, you just needed a man
To fit into your cage, like some master plan

But now I am free girl, unchained by your claws
You held me the hostage, put up marshal laws
You said it was money, you said I was bad
So why do your children still call me their dad
Your walking towards hell, I'm walking towards life

I'll travel the world, talk to God most high

```
                    The Bright Yellow Sign
                    (a waffle house story)
```

it was around two in the morning
i was exhausted and sweaty
i had six dollars in change
and i pulled into the waffle
the bright yellow sign drew me...

as i walked in, i smelt it
that wonderful smell of grease
and flour and teenagers smoking
it was around two in the morning
the bright yellow sign drew me...

i sat down, and the table is sticky
with the syrup of the last customer
there's nick. i order the usual
and start with a bacon sandwich.
that bright yellow sign threw me...

plate after plate, bowl after bowl.
i really think i'm done here
but i can't stand up just yet
i'm not ready for it just yet
that bright yellow sign threw me...

it was around three in the morning
as i staggered out the door
on the way to my car, grabbing a paper
and i think that this time i'm content
that the bright yellow sign was right...

there
on the horizon,
lightning strikes again
and falls crashing
all around
boom
thunder rolls
and fills my lonely heart
with the swift and sure beat
of the wild ever precipitation
sweet rain and the smell of green
wet, ever so wet, rain down
come rain on me, rain
fall and pour
come down
on me
smell of rain
the scent of a new fall
I love, I crave the sound,
and feel the tang and crackle
of it all. Come rain on me rain.
animals hide, but I, much wiser
thrust my heart up to heaven
with my arms outstretched
and open up wide
my mouth and
drink

rain

La la la

Ayatollah has gone the way of the jackal

And the people pray to a setting soul

And wail in Farsi to revive their hearts anew

Whilst dreams die in my heart for 1989

```
                                        NEVER
         (With thanks to the Rabid Oscillating
                                      Weasel)
```

Never pet a burning dog
Never juggle rabid porcupines
Never toy with a polar bears emotions
Never give a stampeding elephant a pedicure
Never tickle a vomiting octopus
Never brush the teeth of a hungry shark
Never sleep next to a grumpy cobra
Never kick a grizzly bear in the eye
Never pee on a silver back gorilla

Never place a rabid squirrel down your pants
    for the purposes of gambling

```
                              Bus Stop
```

Forsaken not forgotten
he stood
she stood
they stood
together
while it rained

and all their thoughts
were as one
were as two
were together
together
while it rained

their love entwined
their souls
their hearts
their minds
as the rain came
and came

lights that came by
shown on
glowed on
splashed on
as they waited there
at the bus stop

and all the while
they waited
they prayed
they hoped
that the bus would
be on time

but they hated
getting wet
so they decided
to share their umbrella
with each other
at the bus stop
until the bus came

Inch by Inch

For He who knows to walk on water need never drown
For She who knows to fly, need never falter
And for they who know to trust, need never fear

Blind faith it was, and always seemed to be
But true faith is always this blind it seems
You, me and Jesus complete
As one sweeps the other of each other's feet

There were two roads their distance untold
Both climbing a mountainous path so old
Each bearing its' traveler, weathered and bruised
Pilgrims of promise, in a barren land used

So inch by slow inch, they walked their course
Ever so slowly towards their common source
And knowing it not, their paths grew to one
And from that day forth, their lives together spun

For He who knows to walk on water need never drown
For She who knows to fly, need never falter
And for they who know to trust, need never fear

Blind faith it was, and always seemed to be
But true faith is always this blind it seems
Me, you and Jesus complete
As one sweeps the other of each other's feet

It's asking for the taking

                                        His house

Expand your imagination,
  open up your heart

Open up your concentration,
  it's not all that hard
Give up all your inner pride,
  and let Jesus in
One simple truth is,
  He's your only true friend
Father to the hurt,
  and home to the beggar
He loves you now today,
  both now and forever
Draw a little door,
  on the doorway of your soul
Open up and let him in,
  to call your house his home.

Spontaneous Psalm #2

Look at the sun
Look at the moon
Look at the stars He's made
How can this come from nothing

Look at the grass on the fields
Look at the flowers
Look at the birds and the bees
If you please

Did it come from nothing
Does it go to nothing
I don't think so
I don't think so

It does not come from nothing
It does not go to nothing
God has a purpose for you

It does not come from nothing

Look at the grass on the fields
Look at the sun in the sky
Look at the way He smiles down upon you

There's a God
It does not go to nothing
It does not come from nothing

You do not come from nothing
You do not go to nothing
Your Father holds you gently
You go to Him

You go to Him
You go to Jesus Christ

He's not nothing
And you are something

You're everything to Him

The true thought

I wonder fully and truly if ever i have wondered false
I imagine clearly and duly if ever imagined wrong
For inside every vessel of trust and languid form
My heart and my mind do collide, despised by logics core

Do you ever, dearest reader, wonder who would dispel
The care taking of little flowers, or a child with the smile of a bell
Or wounding a grounded soldier that desperately needed a lift
Then wonder the dispelling of black against white, for therein is the rift

As evil as a night shroud tomb, as beautiful as the day

Do my inner devils battle each second the angels in their way
If ever the two would agree on one thing, seeing eye to eye
The recourse and final decision must act to that very time

I wonder if ever I fully trust my innards as the poets say
And be true to myself as often as I must, when I often get in my own way
The two hands will join, the battle will cease... I come out on top
But is it right, just and good or is it only evil that is stopped

So decision, torment and strife do haunt, the true believers stance
And regret and remorse do take their recourse, sickles in their hands
The forever battle within me still rages, what I should do or should not do
I know that the locks have broken off their cages, I don't do what I should
do

Will God on his throne, see me here alone questioning every move
I only choose to think that someday soon a savior will appear at high noon
And shoot through my head and kill devils dead i ever hope it now
My morning my cowl my black devil shroud, no more pearls for my sow

Arise once again, my two-headed friend, God almighty my trust
Take once again a piss in the wind, God if you truly must
Call me not again, your lonesome end, for I am only but dust
Count me today as knot on your bends, I in you only will trust

The Foolish Zealot

As I left seminary to go into the new world outside of the college walls, I toyed with a lot of different ideas. The four year program was directly specific for me to be plugged into the "full time ministry" immediately. I did try a bit here and there. I travelled with my snakeskin boot wearing cousin on his preaching circuit, and did several things with other travelling preachers, but I found that I loved the actual setting of the stage and design than the services or the ministries directly connected. More and more I found myself behind the stage at DC Talk, Amy Grant, and the biggest names in Christian Music at the time. Running the monitor mixer or lighting board was more my game than ushering or singing in the choir. That's what got me involved with Gregg Santeen. Gregg and his wife had started a "club" for Christians that featured something that I hadn't heard before, but would soon come to know as my sole staple in music: "Christian Techno." Club Liquid was soon to become my second home. A Christian dance club. Who would have figured?

Not only was I introduced to this new found musical genre, but I was introduced to a whole new style of Christianity. Gregg would introduce me to some of his friends who were not necessarily "churched" but part of the growing number of the unchurched saved. I didn't know these people existed. This new paradigm didn't sit well with me at first. Sure, they might have Bible studies in their home every week, but they didn't go to a building! That really messed with my pre-conceptions. I was still under the notion that going to a big building every Sunday morning meant that Jesus lived in your heart. Cheryl, Gregg's wife responded with: "Where does it say that?" And you know what? I didn't have an answer for her. I fell flat on my theological face, got up, and really started really digging into what the Bible said and how it differed from what man said. Guess what? The teachings of Torah, Jesus himself and the New Testament are in almost diametric polarity from what "American Churchianity" had taught me.

So, before you're ready to venture out on your own theologically, you must begin to question what you've learned. Keith Wheeler had started that journey in me and Gregg had shown me what it looked like in my culture and life. He and his friends would have parties and Bible studies at his house and I was introduced to a neat set of people who I had previously thought were not in existence. Around this time, I took my first "ministry" job at 55th Street Church. The budget wasn't large, but the pastor's two sons and one of the women on the church board were all teenagers so suddenly it was a priority. With a gang of eight unruly mobsters and myself we set about learning the ways of the Bible. Every now and again we would do something special, but it was small time. I think I may have been there to babysit. But we dug into the word and made it applicable. You have to change one life at a time and I was doing just that. Nothing complicated, nothing special. Just a youth pastor at a small church doing small things for God.

If you haven't discerned by now I guess you can take a guess that I don't have a shred of anything like decency. I was more of a radical if anything. So get this… Our church was right next door to a middle school, and it was right down the road from the local high school. Talk about an opportunity. So I got this wild hair and I figured if I had some way to lure those children over to the church I could preach the gospel to them. I talked to the church pastor about it and he kind of laughed and said: "Go for it." So I did. I knew that Tuesdays were a pretty dull day for everything, so I printed up a flyer. "The Hangout" was open right after school. Free games, free snacks, loud music, basketball and fun. I took a stack over to the assistant principal and asked him what he thought. He took a look at me and said: "Go for it." So I left the flyers at the principal's office and left with a smile.

Word got out. One of those uber busybodies moms found a flyer who circulated it to her friends and wouldn't you know it, it was a hit. I hadn't expected what happened to happen. Let me explain: 55th Street Church had around 30 people in regular attendance on any given Sunday. Mostly it comprised of the aged. And the few families that weren't near their death bed had children in my youth group. It was small, small minded, and a *we're doing just fine as we are thank-you-very-much* type of church. So. When I opened the side doors to the building, turned up the music to a deafening level, and threw Little Debbie snacks at them, things went bonkers. Like the ocean, the entire downstairs was flooded with maniacs running around eating snacks, downing Kool-Aid and hitting up the few console games I had hooked up. Soon enough, there was a full on basketball game in our parking lot with a surging crowd going ballistic. Then, the pastor appeared at my elbow. Sure, he had gotten my note about "The Hangout" but this was *NOT* what he had in mind. The very next day an emergency steering committee had been formed and I was drowned in red tape.

I will give the pastor credit. He was my only cheerleader in that meeting. The old ladies got together and decided to break out the popcorn machine they had in the basement and take turns "helping." Figuratively, with minds blown they had seen their church do something wonderful. It was unforeseeable to them, literally incomprehensible, but what were they to do but react in a manner that one does in the face of an oncoming hurricane? They bit their lips, rolled up their sleeves, and got to work. Oh. And they made me turn down the music. They wrote me an itinerary: Bring in the kids, let them play games for 10 minutes, gather them up for a 2 minute Bible study, a 15 second prayer for their souls, then let them play for another 45 minute. Parent after parent would come to hang out with their sons and daughters and chit-chat about Christian goings-on, the weather and recipes. Soon enough, we were down to thirty or forty kids. Then, twenty or so. The move that God had intended had been quickly suffocated by the hand of man.

God is so huge, so magnificent, and so lovely that we think we know what He wants and what He is. We grow up with "the way things are" and never challenge our boundaries. Why is this? What is the fear? Are we afraid of what we will find out? I've never taken these two lessons for granted. I always wanted to find the fresh hand of what God was doing. I've always wanted to be a part of it. I've always wanted the *Ruach*, the fresh breath. I stayed on at the church a little while longer, just enough to become dead inside, until I decided that I would rather be with my girlfriend who was in Indiana. So, I gave up, gave everything away, moved up, married her, and began anew.

Ultimate Truth

Ultimate truth is Jesus Christ. There is no other way to say it. He was the only true being. For if truth is the embodiment of God, then He was the first of many. As the first of many born from the dead infused with the power of God, so are the sons and daughters of God when they have Christ within.

We who live here in America call ourselves Americans… meaning that we live in America. I as a person who lives in Christ call myself a Christian. For one to acknowledge ultimate truth, I must acknowledge Him who sent it. That Person is Jesus Christ.

There is no other man who walked the crust of this earth to claim that. From the five major branches of religion we have only one who has ever fulfilled prophesy to the extreme that Christ did. We see in Christianity, Judaism, and Islam God depicted as "El" (translated "Al" in Arabic). He is seen as supreme, eternal and the composite of all truth. Within these three major monotheistic (meaning: one God) religions, we are all seen as the children of Adam, Noah, and Abraham. The only difference is that within the bounds of Christianity we are able to become one with the creator of the cosmos. We are to be friends with the Truth.

Buddhism and Hinduism hold that all incarnation is God. Rocks, trees, angels, cows, clouds, butterflies… these all hold spirits of the deity. Everything is "god". They believe that all lives are subjective to the greatness of everything. They see that there are as many truths in the cosmos as there are molecules, and they are all valid and of equal importance. Christianity however has a much different viewpoint. We see lower beings as who they are, created things in the spirit of the Creator. Angels are not god themselves but they are Elohim. They are a secondary spiritual power. Whether still in the service of God or not, they are not god in themselves. Fallen spirits have the mane given to them of "devils". We do not worship them, we worship the one who made them, and who made everything.

Judaism waits for its messiah. Islam has had more than five messiahs, but Christianity holds Jesus Christ as the only and true Messiah. For over thirty years, from physical birth to ascension, Jesus Christ performed over forty miracles, fulfilled over twenty major prophesies, and even raised three people from the dead (including himself). In contrast, Islam's Mohammed only fulfilled one prophesy, did no miracles, and raised no one from the dead. The prophesy he fulfilled? He stated "I will return to Mecca." Easy one. You or I could do that. There's not much power behind that.

As we discussed in a previous chapter, the sum of his words are truth. That brings us to the canonized Bible, what we commonly call the sixty-six books (really seventy books... Psalms is a collection of five books). Genesis to Revelation. Excluding the Apocrypha of course.

At the canonization, different books were tossed around, different views held. The Gospel of Thomas, The secret writings of John, Polycarp's Epistles, The book of Enoch, Ecclesiasticus...etc... Those in charge of the selections entered into the task of selecting the ones with great care and prayer. The canonization was fasted over and prayed over heavily. All men believed these books to be the only books to be included in the word of God for all people. There was a rumor of a man who believed a certain book to be included in the word, and announced to those assembled that if it wasn't to be included in the Bible, that he was to be struck dead by God himself. The next day he was found dead... having expired in his sleep of natural causes.

We know our Bible exists today as God breathed and inspired. There were over forty authors writing over a one thousand year period about the same thing. The Truth of God. Amos was a farmer. Moses was an outlaw. Solomon was a king. Peter was a fisherman, and Paul was a rabbi... All from walks of life and yet, as a whole, the Bible has changed and affected more lives than any book ever made.

Still holding the number one place in three categories... The number one book ever sold or bought, the most read book in all of history, and the most stolen book in history. In any language, in any translation, version or paraphrase, the Bible calls out to men both far and wide begging to be read and understood.

Do we dare to confront this book with our own puny opinion? Like Jim Jones, throw the book down to the floor declaring that we have reached a point in our own personal theology that we no longer need it? Do we do as Benjamin Franklin did, and cut out the parts that offend us? Ha. My friend, I for one would rather tie a boulder around my neck and pray that rocks float as I cast myself into the ocean than to take anything away from the Word of God.

Ultimate truth is Jesus Christ. Ultimate truth is found in the word, for as John says in the gospel of John, chapter one, verse fourteen: And the word became flesh and lived among us. The great Apostle Paul strove to know nothing but Christ and him crucified. Even Jesus Christ said of himself: I am the bread of life, He who comes to me need never hunger, and he who believes in me need never thirst.

By the Gates of the Garden of Eden

Just as the idea for Empires and Generals had come upon me after doing research into the Terra Cotta Army, the idea for my first novel came upon me while also doing research. It had been really five years since my last deep creative effort into anything and, although I loved diving into weird parts of history and really mapping it all out and then turning it into an educational game, I was hungry for something original. I was working 15 hours a day at two jobs and was still newly married, but that hole in my heart where creativity longed to be born was growing moldy and sour. It was 2012 and I had reworked the Mayan Calendar into a modern day working one (just in case the world ended,) so that filled a little bit of the need, but not enough. I love massive projects, and small ones are just "breaks" from the larger ones. As it happened, I was watching "The Office" in when Dwight Schrute dresses as Belsnickel, and I was inspired to do a little light research on the subject of Christmas history and folklore.

Several months later I came out of my writing closet with a rough outline of a manuscript. It would later evolve into By the Gates of the Garden of Eden. It's the tale a college guy who gets kidnapped by Krampus, made to work in a cave, escapes, and leads his friends to freedom. That's the gist of the novel. Just like any novel it has ups and downs, good-guys and bad-guys and an exciting ending. But the subject matter was born of some "deep truth" stuff. What had begun in German Christmas folklore had come out on the other end looking more like a who's-who of Conspiracy theories. *Deep Underground Military Bases, Ancient Aliens, Secret Societies, Antediluvian*

Man, *Nephilim Hybrids*, *Genetic Manipulation*, *Giants*, *Cryptozoology*, and of course, *Flat Earth*. It was pretty amazing and helped me discover much of what I was working towards: understanding the last plans for Satan and his minions for the end of the age.

I took a little time after the publication to firm up what I believed in the flat earth, but more importantly just how deep the cover-up went to delude modern man away from its reality. I found evidence for the militaries of the world to shoo us away from Antarctica, found evidence to delude us into believing in NASA's claims for extra-terrestrial life, and a host of others. It was thrilling to dive head first into the rabbit hole, drink the drink-me drink and crawl thru the smallest door. What was the purpose of the saints at the end of the age? We were still supposed to make disciples right? Yes, I determined, but we should make smart ones. I was convinced of the verse more and more that we should be as wise as serpents but harmless as doves. "With the Bible in one hand and a newspaper in the other," Karl Barth said we should be prepared. He referred to the fact that for too long, we as the ecclesia of Christ have used our faith as a ticket out of this world, instead of a reason to engage it. But I am the chiefest of sinners in this regard. I hunker down in my office and bury myself with Sumerian Tablets and Mayan Calendars and say: "I'm doing God's work!" When instead I should be telling others about Him. Eh, I don't know. There's a balance somewhere out there as a writer, maybe I just don't know it yet.

I will say this on the subject of digging into truth. Whereas I had built my imaginary galaxy for ten years and had all my little alien ducks in a row ready to write my novel series, it is way more satisfying to dig into truth on my own and fill in the gaps with fun. Writing a novel about real possibilities (read: Speculative Fiction) has become more of a satisfying adventure than what the Bible calls: "Vain Imaginations" – for vanity should be nailed to the cross and allowed to suffocate there, along with all sin... For the blood of Christ is a propitiation for all of man's shortcomings including pride of achievement, vanity and all lures of the enemy over our lives. Everyone has a deep sin seed. Whether it is self, power, sex, money, or whatever; we all have a weakness that needs to be placed at the feet of our Intelligent Designer. For if He is, and we are His design, then certainly He knows our flaws, our weaknesses, just as much as He knows our strengths and attributes. Just as He has the power to create the known cosmos, He has the power to love it...

Including us as His primary creation. For we are the only creation to be made in His image. We are the only part of creation to look like He who made us. This fact should blow us away every single second.

And no matter what we do on our own, whether it's as unimportant as making a really snappy Facebook comeback, or as important as birthing a child, we should remember that we are but inventors. He alone is the creator. For invention is making something from something else. I'm not going to "create" anything really... Right? But YHVH, YHWH, Elohim, El, Yah – He is the one who actually creates. He alone "makes," He is the only divine uncreated, for He created all things. And that's what we need to remember. We can find "His Story" (History) and acknowledge His divinity in it and come to grips with the facts that surround all of the mysteries in this world, but we are only uncovering what was already there. We are only archeologists, rediscovering what may have been lost in the first place. But now that we have found it, we become responsible for knowing it. And that's quite a responsibility.

Come let's go

dear church:

when the little box was checked and the little card was dropped into the bucket three weeks ago i didn't realize the impact that it would have on my life. pastor brad had just gotten through exhorting us to try to do our best to follow along at home on this new teaching adventure: chasing daylight. i, for one, have never been a proponent of homework, but was strangely compelled to do just that very thing. to go buy the book, read one chapter a week, and attend my small group to discuss what we had all been experiencing. well, things were working smoothly on that front. my wife and i had been keeping our end of the bargain waiting on God to show us why we had signed up in the first place. i mean. i can get God just the same without a little book, can't i?

come let's go. come let us go. whether three words or four, they have been running through my head for over a month now. it has been a bit tricky at times to fit it into our schedules, but, i imagine we have all had that as either an excuse or a reason to not do anything that we promise to do. last week we fell behind a little in the reading part of it, so we found ourselves "cramming" before our small group started with chapter three. the weekly readings of "chasing daylight" by erwin mcmanus have been meaningful and thought-provoking thus far, but it had not impacted our lives until this week. it all started on sunday.

on sunday i proposed to do such a thing. something that had "come let's go" written on it. my wife and i are both givers and we were both seeking God on who to bless with a "monetary surprise" and we happened to decide on the same person and almost the same amount. having her and i agree on money was indeed a miracle, so we decided to go for it. so, using stealth and love, we sprang our blessing on our unsuspecting victim after church service sunday and departed with the happiness that can only be felt through doing something awesome. it was more than we even usually put in the offering bucket, but we felt good about things. it even fit neatly into our budget for the month. hey, what could be better?

things were even happy when my beautiful wife decided to take the day off monday so that we could run down to the tag agency and work on our quote "car stuff" as i like to call it. things were not so happy thirty minutes later when the total bill for our "car stuff" had topped off at around a thousand dollars. no kidding. a thousand bucks.

after leaving the tag agency with empty wallets, fuzzy brains and weakened resolve there seemed to be a black hand that came up from the horizon and loomed over us. even the drive home, usually five minutes seemed like a journey across the great state of kansas that lasted an entire day. i immediately became fearful and disenchanted with Gods perfect plan for my life and argumentative towards my wife. things were looking bleak. severely bleak indeed. i could have really used a heads up God.

so now we have no money. besides the gas in our cars and the change bucket we had at the house. we had no money. rent was due on the first, and we hadn't even bought our bi-weekly groceries. we need oranges, we need bread. we need milk.

and so the week went. we cooked leftovers and visited exciting websites that promised a cuisine out of three potatoes and a tablespoon of cooking oil. it was time to get inventive. it was time to stand firm in our faith, it was time to believe in the promises of God for our lives. so what did we do? yeah. we mostly did just that. i would like to give this great story a twist and tell you how i climbed up in the crows nest and had a lieutenant dan moment, but no. this story is nothing like that. we just relaxed and trusted Jesus. it was pretty cool.

and here is why:

number one: we were obedient when God told us to bless those people.

number two: we had "done something". we said to each other: "come let's go" and decided to let God determine the outcome.

number three: we trusted Him with our giving. no pomegranate tree-sitters here. we had one sword and were going to use it.

well so now our story comes to a close. i'll bet you are guessing what comes next. were they able to pay rent? did God come through? what happened? ooh i'll bet the suspense is killing you.

yes. God came through. and he answered in a way that makes a great ending to this little story. over the course of this week, unexpectedly, God has had four different people sow food and money into our lives. over three hundred dollars. we can now pay rent, buy some oranges and some bread, and hold each other reassuringly knowing that God is in His throne, His son is standing next to Him interceding for us, and His Spirit, the hope of Glory, resides in us, comforting us in everything.

oh look, the mailman just got here. guess what just arrived. some coupons for free milk.

isn't God amazing?

www.ingramcontent.com/pod-product-compliance
Lightning Source LLC
Chambersburg PA
CBHW030153200626
46812CB00016B/1830